<u>ACKNOWLEDGEMENTS</u>

I would like to thank my kids for being so patient with me throughout all that we have been through, my mother KK for always having my back, Ms. Alice for being a second mom to me and keeping me in check. I would not have been able to accomplish or get through some rough shit in my life without loving family and friends. I appreciate Eric so much for being my rib and keeping me level headed. Mr. Sean Wright you are so fuckin dope; without you I would not be looking at my first book of many.

Thank you all,

~Brook Rich

BROKEN BROOKLYNN BRIDGES By Jersi K. Lee

PROLOGUE

"Yo remember what I said; keep the car running, in gear, and your foot on the break until I get back in." Black Tone said getting out of the car and heading into the West Philly National Bank.

I probably should have been scared to death, but the truth of the matter is I had ice in my veins and no fear. I just sat there doin what I was told while I smoked what was left of a coke filled blunt, and blasting the new Lil Kim record. I was lost in my thoughts and having visions of grandeur about what my life would be like when Black Tone came out of the bank. First thing I was gonna do was put a down payment on a house for my mom so she could get better and we could get up out of the hood. I was also gonna buy myself mad Ed Hardy and Juicy Couture shit and I was gonna be the most talked about chick in the hood. I could see it all, and my mouth watered at the thought of a major life change being less than 4 minutes away.

I was boppin my head and grinning from ear to ear when I heard shots ring out. At first I paid it no mind and kept doing me. After all I was listening to Lil Kim and gun shots in her music were common. It wasn't until I heard the screaming that I snapped out of my trance and saw Black Tone come busting out of the bank headed for the car. Although he had a duffle bag full of cash the look on his face said that things had gone terribly wrong. It was crazy because he was running top speed, yet he appeared to be running in slow motion. I aint gonna lie, it took everything in me not to pull the fuck off, but Black Tone was an O.G. in Philly and the repercussions of doing such a thing would be vital.

After what appeared to be a lifetime Tone had made it to the car. He opened the door and then dropped. I never heard the shot, but his brains all over the dash and my face proved that there had been one. I punched the gas and took off, dragging Black Tone's lifeless body more than half a block before it detached itself from the door hinge. I was frantic, and the tears flooding my eyes made driving at full speed impossible. After turning the corner and losing control I crashed into a light pole, climbed out of the car and hauled ass without looking back. What a hell of a way to spend my 13th birthday.

CHAPTER 1

I grew up in a small town in Pennsylvania called Coatesville. It was so small that everybody knew everybody so everybody was fucking everybody. It was nasty, but that was life in the hood. It wasn't always like that for me; my mother was pregnant with me when she was only seventeen. In her hay day my mom was the shit; she was slim with thick black hair, and beautiful Cherokee skin. Everybody was on my mom, but her heart and virginity went to her high school boyfriend who was also the star of the football team. As fate would have it that relationship would get rocky and soon come to an end, but that definitely didn't slow moms down. At six months pregnant she found her way backstage at a Levert concert with her older sisters and that's where she met Levert's road manager A.B. Mom wasn't showing so A.B. didn't know about me right away, but when he did find out he didn't flinch a bit. He assumed the role of my father married my mom and has been my dad ever since.

Two years later mom gave birth to my sister Bianca in Cleveland Ohio; we had relocated there for a while and again life as I knew it was totally lit. But living that life came with a price; my dad was a great provider, but he was always on the road, and him being gone so much caused him and my mom to fight a lot, so not too long after mom gave birth to my brother Adam, her and dad divorced. That crushed me, and that's when life as I knew it took a total turn for the worse.

"Brooklynn, bring mommy her special bag." My mother yelled from her bed as I rolled my eyes, sucked my teeth, got up from doing Bianca's hair and headed to the kitchen.

When I got to the kitchen I grabbed a stool and pushed it up against the fridge so that I was tall enough to reach the velvet like Crown Royal bag my mom kept up there. It had been years since her and dad divorced, but mom was still taking it hard, and when she couldn't have dad she found another lover; alcohol. With mom drinking heavy the way she was I quickly and suddenly became the woman of the house at 14 years old. I cooked, cleaned, and took care of Mom, Bianca, and Adam. In all honesty I would have preferred to be a normal kid, but mom just wasn't the same when we moved back to Coatesville after the divorce. I aint gonna lie, this regular livin shit was wack as fuck, but I was forced to roll with the punches at an early age.

"Here mom." I said handing her the bottle as she sat up in her bed and feeling around for it without even removing the Gucci eye mask that she seemed to wear almost all day as she slept and drank the days away. Yeah, she stayed getting bent, but she was still bougie as fuck.

"That's a good girl. What is your brother and sister doing?" She asked while taking a long swig from the bottle while still not lifting the eye cover.

"They're fine mom; Adam is eating dinner, and Bianca is waiting for me to finish her hair so she can take a shower and get ready for bed, and Adam will follow when he is done eating."

"What would I do without you baby?" She slurred.

"I don't know mom. I really don't know." I said taking the bottle from her, and placing it on the nightstand as she slowly eased back onto her pillow and dozed back off."

I kissed her on the cheek, turned off her night lamp, and exited the room; it was getting late and the kids had to be in bed. The kids; that shit sounded funny as hell as if I wasn't just a kid my motherfuckin self.

<u>CHAPTER 2</u>

"Bianca, Adam let's go. You're gonna be late for school." I yelled up the stairs.

"Be quiet Brook, you gonna wake mom." Bianca said heading downstairs with Adam in tow.

"Girl please. There could be an earthquake and mom wouldn't budge." I mumbled under my breath.

"Bwooklynn can we stop for ice cream?" Adam asked putting on his knapsack.

"What? Boy no, now let's go. I swear if ya'll late for school I'm whoopin ass when ya'll get home." I said pulling on Bianca as she pulled on Adam.

I was damn near pulling them down the street so that they wouldn't be late. It was bad enough we had to walk 2 miles every day because mom didn't turn in the bus pass application on time. It was all good, I aint care if we had to walk 20 miles a day I would not stand for Bianca or Adam being late to school. I was really serious about their education and slacking was not tolerated.

Almost an hour later we arrived in front of the school.

"Aight ya'll know the drill. Bianca you walk Adam to his class and get straight to yours. Adam you behave, no more temper tantrums or dat ass is mine when you get home. Do you understand me?" I said sternly.

"Yes Brooklyyn." They said in unison.

"Aight now give me a kiss and hug."

They both happily did as instructed as I returned the gesture and turned to walk away.

"Hey Brook. How come you get to skip school whenever you want to? Bianca asked.

"Cuz somebody gotta help mom take care of ya'll rug rats. I'll be back to get ya'll at three. " I said rushing trying to get off school property before I got caught.

Minutes later I walked into Jason's store/weed spot, passed the cashier, and headed straight to the back. When I got to the large steel door I knocked three short times. Seconds later Jason's security guard Fat Ronnie opened the door.

"What's good Brook?" He said looking me up and down while licking his black weed smoker's lips.

"Wassup Ronnie." I said ignoring his perverted gestures. Motherfucker musta forgot that although I got thick as fuck over the Summer I was still only 14 years old.

I pushed passed him and headed over to where Jason was bagging up my morning package.

"Wassup lil bit?" He said putting the last 20 sack together and dropping it into the brown paper bag that contained the rest of the work.

"Ready to get on my grind as usual." I said taking the package from him.

"That's my little soldier." He said patting me on my back.

"I'll be back before I go pick the kids up from school." I said putting the package into my book bag.

"No doubt. You be careful out there."

"Always." I said pushing passed Fat Ronnie again and leaving out to earn money for the household.

You would think that after that shit went down last year with Black Tone I woulda chilled out, but just the thought of what was in that bag he was carrying actually turned me on. I was literally 30 seconds away from having enough money to change my family's lives before Tone got his wig pushed back, and I wanted that feeling again. This time I would be way safer though.

I wasn't on the block five minutes before the potheads started callin me out.

"Yo Brook lemme get a dub sack."

That shit was like music to my ears. Getting paid was all about supply and demand. I was learning that a young age and it would prove to be one of life's greatest lessons. I was clearing about a hundred a day after paying Jason back and at 14 that shit was like $100,000.00.

After trapping for a few hours, picking the kids up, and dropping them off I went to see my aunt Sandy. She was like my damn therapist. She knew all the shit I was dealing with and how much of a strain it was on me, but she also knew I was keeping it together and holding the crib down; she just didn't know how and I damn sure wasn't about to tell her the truth.

"Hey Auntie." I said walking into her house and kissing her on the cheek.

"Heeeey baby. How are you feeling? Come on sit down and tell me all about it." She said patting the worn down sofa next to her.

Truth be told I really didn't have any shocking new developments, I mean I used to cry to her about how fucked up life was after moving back to Coatesville, and how I missed A.B., but struggled with the fact that my real father never reached out to me. There were times when I was just a ball of mixed emotions, but I would never let my mom and my siblings see me in that state. I was the oldest and I had to be strong. However, I often suppressed my hurt and kept it bottled up. I aint need Aunt Sandy to diagnose me; I'm sure that's most if not all of the reason the rest of my life became a roller coaster of bullshit.

CHAPTER 3

In middle school I was really feelin myself. I was a young, thick, bad, redbone bitch that was getting money. I mean you couldn't tell me shit. You name the latest fashions and I had it. I also had the attention of damn near every nigga in The Ville and I loved it. I no longer had to hustle because mom was getting better, and I was such a bad bitch all I had to do was breath in the direction of something I wanted and there would be 20 niggas trying to be the first to get it.

Even at such a young age I started seeing this married dude whose name I won't mention for obvious reasons. Our relationship was crazy we broke up seven damn times and got back together. He was the cutest and sweetest Puerto Rican, but things quickly died down between us. We ended on a good note; we are actually good friends till this day. I dated a few guys after him, but in 7th grade my whole life changed.

I had gone to a High School football game with my cousin Alona. Ever since mom had gotten herself together she actually became the mom of the house again and started acting accordingly. I guess she could see the direction I was headed in and tried her best to keep me on a short leash. So there were not many places she would allow me to go; however she didn't mind me being with my big cousin. Little did she know I got into even more trouble with my cousin than when I was on my own. Anyway back to this boy; I had to have him at any cost. Just the sight of his long curly hair made me feel like it was love at first site. The fucked up thing about it was he was super popular and all the girls wanted him so I knew I didn't have a chance. For the first time ever I felt intimidated and I was like a fish out of water. I was never nervous to bag any nigga because I always allowed them to bag me.

"Damn Brook put your eyes back in ya damn head." Alona said noticing me staring.

"Yo cuz. Who the fuck is that?" I asked sounding more thirsty than I actually wanted to.

"That's Corey Holmes. I'mma hook you up."

She grabbed my hand and led me over towards him. My heart was beating out of my chest while my stomach did cartwheels. What the fuck was the foreign feeling I was having.

"Yo Corey. This my little cousin Brooklynn. Fuck all these other hoes you dealin with. Brooklynn will shit on every last one of 'em any day of the week." Alona said looking the group of girls surrounding Corey dead in the eye.

"She dope as fuck, but she look kinda young." Corey said giving me the once over.

"She aint jailbait young nigga. Stop bein so scary and make ya next move ya best move."

"Aight. Well slide me her number then, and I'mma holla at her."

"Why the fuck are ya'll talkin bout me like I aint standin the fuck right here?" I said snapping out of my trance.

"Aww shit. She a dime and she got some fire with her. I love it." Corey said flashing the most beautiful smile I had ever seen in my young ass life.

I pulled a pen out of my Juicy Couture purse and wrote my number on the palm of his hand.

"Use it or lose it .C'mon cuz." I said really feelin myself at this point.

And just like that I had my baby and them bitches hated it with a passion. Here was this much younger bitch with the nigga they was all dyin to bust it open for and ever since he met me he never looked them hoes way again. However, once again as my pattern and track record would prove that shit didn't last either. As much as we loved, cherished, and understood each other the hate, ridicule, rumors, and fights with his fan club was becoming too much for my mind to bare. We started having issues, I just prayed we could make it through the bullshit because I loved Corey with every ounce of my soul.

<u>CHAPTER 4</u>

It was New Year's Eve and I had just turned 16 not even 24 hours earlier. I went to see my aunt and cousins in Philly. I got with my cousins and they took me to some guy's crib who was having a New Years Eve Party. It was an adult party so they sent us kids upstairs. It was me, my three cousins, and some other young boy who was in town visiting his uncle from Trinidad.

We were all playing cards when I asked for something to drink.

"No doubt shorty. I'll be right back." One of the guys said as he headed downstairs.

Before I knew it he was back with a large bottle of E&J he had snuck away from the adults downstairs who were obviously too drunk to notice.

"Now this is a party?" He said while pouring shots for everybody.

I wasn't a drinker or smoker at that age, but I was with my big cousins so I was like "Fuck it" when you with the big girls, you gotta be a big girl. With that being said, I started downing shots like everybody else.

After only the second shot I felt dizzy, sick and needed to lie down. The next thing I knew some old man comes in with one of them old ass cameras complete with the big ass flash and all and snapped a picture of me. Then another guy comes in right after that and throws me over his fuckin shoulder caveman style talking about he was going to lay me down. Meanwhile I could feel him touching me all over my body. Never have I felt so fuckin helpless. He took me in another room, laid me down, and told me to rest as he left and turned out the lights.

"Thank God." I thought to myself.

But then another guy came in and immediately started getting asshole naked.

"Yo. What are you doing?" I slurred.

He didn't respond. He just jumped on me and started taking off my clothes. I tried to scream but he his hand covering my mouth forced my voice back down my throat. I was crying and begging him to stop, but my pleads fell on deaf ears. I suddenly looked over on the nightstand and saw a lighter. I lit it and tried to burn him, but he knocked it out of my hand. I bit his hand and screamed, but the music from the party drowned my cries for help. No one could hear me, but no one came looking for their little cousin either.

When I woke up my body was sore and I was bloody all over. I stumbled to the bathroom and saw a hickey the size of a globe on my neck. I slid down the bathroom wall and started to cry. For a youngin I had dated my fair share of men, but I was still a virgin and in love. So how was I supposed to explain this to Corey? He was supposed to be my first. A million thoughts raced through my mind. Was this my fault? Did I do something to provoke this? I cried hoping my tears would hit the floor and spell out the answer, but to no avail. Here was the pattern again; another chapter in my so young yet so fucked up life.

<u>CHAPTER 5</u>

It took me six months to tell my mom what happened that dreadful night. I was afraid that she would think I was lying and my little hot ass just gave myself up to my boyfriend. My thoughts could not have been farther from the truth. For the first time in a long time my mother cried, nurtured me, and became my protector. From that point on she was afraid for me to even leave the house. My boyfriend on the other hand doesn't believe my story to this day. He thinks I cheated but fuck him. I know what the hell happened.

You would think that after being raped I would become more reserved, but the effect was the absolute opposite. I became so sexual and fast it was crazy. My sexual beast was untamed and I couldn't get it back in the cage. I started fucking with guys I knew I had no business with. My head was all fucked up. The older I got, the more shapely I got. As a young teen I was shaped like a brick shit house and put most old head broads to shame. I always wore my hair in braids or a wrap to accentuate my chinky eyes. Guys always thought I was Asian or Hawaiian.

It wasn't long before I met this dude from New Jersey I'll call him Mikey. Mikey was a bad boy and by now I had a thing for bad boys. Oh did I mention I was also dealing with someone else at that time with my little fast ass? I'll call him…aww what the fuck does it matter at this point? I was young, dumb, naïve and I didn't care. What I did care about was one of them niggas got me pregnant and I had no idea which one it was. So here I was pregnant at 16. Oddly enough my mom wanted me to keep it, but I was young and selfish. No fuckin way I wanted to be tied down with a kid and I was just a kid myself. So I went and got an abortion; truth be told that shit still haunts me to this day.

My pregnancy must have been contagious because Mom ended up pregnant and having a baby girl named Cora. She was a beautiful and amazing little girl; her father not so much.

****
****

I started getting blocked calls on the house phone all times of night from some nigga that said he got my number from a friend, and that he really liked me. Like a jackass I started entertaining the shit. You know me, always a sucker for attention. It was fun for a while, but shit started to get weird. This nigga started calling just to masturbate to the sound of my voice. I would hang up and he would call back to back. I begged for him to stop so I wouldn't get into any trouble.

"Let me finish and I won't call back." He would respond.

So I would let him finish and hang up. This shit went one every night for weeks then I just started answering the phone and putting it down. I knew the routine buy now; same time every night. But one day he called when I wasn't home with his sick ass. I was away for the weekend and my mom called to ask if I was okay because she had gotten his calls. So I came home and came clean. She freaked out and called the police immediately who told us to dial *67 if he called back in order to trace the call. I remember thinking at that very moment "technology is the shit".

We waited for him to call back, did as we were instructed and all jaws hit the ground when the call was traced back to Cora's dad. My sister was too young for us to tell her at that time, but the perverted deed also went ignored. Once again I had more fucked up shit to bury deep inside my mental as if it never happened. But God don't like ugly. Cora's dad turned out to be a deadbeat and ended up on the sex offenders list for some other weird and sick shit he was doing. My sister on the other hand, turned out to be a wonderful strong female. She is now a beautiful and smart makeup artist. (do that shit sis)

<u>CHAPTER 6</u>

After all that weird shit mom decided it was time for a change so she packed us up and moved us to Houston, Texas. That shit was a fucking culture shock out of this world for us, but it was beautiful and I loved every bit of it. I had an aunt and some cousins there already so that made the transition a little easier and things were good....for a minute.

Not long after the move I ended up meeting these girls. They were the "hot girls" in town. They knew everybody and everybody knew them. So you know "Good Ole Brooklyyn" had to meet a guy. We'll call this one Jon. Jon was definitely eye candy. He was also a smooth talker, and I was feeling every bit of him. He was tall and paper bag brown with curly hair, perfectly arched eyebrows, a shape up tighter than fish pussy, and the most heavenly green eyes. F.Y.I. I'm a sucker for pretty eyes even till this day. He was well spoken, had a nice car, had some bread and could sing his ass off. I was like "shit. I aint been here a week yet and hit the fuckin jackpot already." Once again life as I knew it was great, but if you have been paying attention you knew that sit wasn't gonna last long.

Mom ended up getting sick. I'm not talking about coughs and sniffles type of sick. I'm talking about REAL sick. We didn't know what was wrong. It turned out that's the reason why we made this big move so that she could find better doctors to help her. She needed somebody to tell her what was going on. It was so bad that at times we thought she wouldn't make it. She wasn't getting out of bed, she was losing weight, always cold, body sore, but she was string so she always made sure we were good. I still had to step in like always to protect her and my siblings. Well it was just me and my two sisters. My brother was with my father in Ohio.

Jon turned out to be super helpful. He would take us to school, grocery shopping, whatever we needed. I really just wanted to be friends, but Jon fell in love with me. It was making me uncomfortable and I knew I needed to just part ways with him, but I knew I needed him around to help. (looking back in it, maybe I was subconsciously using him a little bit). But the nice guy I met became a fuckin wcirdo. He just out of the blue started doin strange shit. He was stopping me form going to school, wanting me around him all damn day. I aint really think nothing of it because "once again" I was with an older boy who was showing me a great time. Until he started being obsessed and telling me I wasn't allowed to see anyone else, but fuck that, I aint care how he felt. If I wanted to do me then that's exactly what the hell I was gonna do. I really started to like him, but his antics were becoming too much for me to handle.

In my travels with he same group of girls, I ended up meeting yup you guessed it, another nigga. His name was Teazi and his swag so on a hundred and I was immediately hooked. He was totally different from Jon. We were never sexual, we just enjoyed each other. He didn't have a car or money so I kept Jon around for those reasons.

My mom was still sick and we still didn't know what was going on. I often prayed for her to get better so I could be a regular kid. But because of her condition I needed to keep Jon around and I hated it. Teazie knew about Jon and he didn't like him one bit. I explained the situation and he understood. I loved Teazie because all he ever wanted to do was protect me. He never wanted anything else. My mom hated Jon too. She swore up and down that he was trying to kill her. I often laughed it off and told her that he was simply there to help us out. Deep down I knew the nigga was a little off. I mean at times I really thought his cheese was sliding off his cracker, but never in a million years did I think he was that crazy.

Jon never hit me; he was a different type of scary. He was the type to lock me in the room for hours, or wait till im washing clothes and steal the clothes out the washer and blame it on someone else just so I couldn't go outside. Then he would "miraculously" recover the stolen items to make himself look like some damn hero; fuckin nut. One time the nigga threw himself off a two story building just to get my attention. I'm tellin ya'll he did weirdo shit like bangin on my window with a pot and pan if I didn't after my phone after the 100th time he tried to call just to make me come outside and have sex with him. This nigga made my nerves bad and had me totally shot the fuck out. This nigga had to go.

CHAPTER 7

One day Jon had me skip school, he took me to his moms house and handed me a pregnancy test out of the blue and forced me to take it. My heart dropped as it came back positive. I locked the bathroom door and cried my eyes out. Now I was stuck with this crazy bastard because I refused to get another abortion as the last one still haunted me from time to time. And while I'm crying my eyes out, this fool sits down and start playing the piano screaming PRAISE THE LORD! He knew he had me on lock now.

Three months into the pregnancy and nobody is happy but dumb ass Jon. I mean my baby was coming so I was happy to be a mom, just not to that nut. You would think that as happy as he was that he would change, but that shit aint happen. In all actuality he just got even worse than before. He was so obsessed that he rented the apartment right under ours. It freaked us all out so mom moved us to a different complex all together.

After a while things started looking up. Me and Jon were no longer together and mom was getting better. I had gotten job at a Mcdonald's that was walking distance from home. I was making a lil money, my family was happy and life was starting to look up once again.

I had met these rappers that lived a few doors down (no. I ant fuck none of em) they were more like my brothers. Jon scary ass was afraid of them so he wouldn't step foot in the complex, he would just come and harass me at work begging me to take him back. It felt so good not to need him, but I was still carrying his child. I actually felt bad for the guy. It must have been my hormones or something.

One day he called and said he wanted to take me for ice cream. When he pulled up I was talking to a guy friend of mine from the complex. When I jumped in the car Jon was cool, but as soon as we pulled off this nut started beating on the steering wheel.

"You wanna play with me? Who was that you was talkin to? You know what? I'mma show you."

I was trying to explain myself when Jon punched on the gas and started speeding down the parking lot at top speed, but before we reached the complex exit I dove out of the car. (yes, at 4 months pregnant). Of course he stopped the car and started apologizing. He always seemed so sincere when he wasn't upset. I told him to leave and I went home, started rubbing my belly and crying. I wanted a family, and I didn't want a baby without a father. What the fuck was I gonna do?

CHAPTER 8

The situation with Jon was upsetting mom and making her sick again, so she decided it was best to move back to Pennsylvania. My rebellious was about to have a baby girl who I would name Jersi and she needed her father. I knew he was crazy, but in my mind Jon had never hit me so it wasn't all that bad. I will say this; he loved the idea of having another daughter. He already had another daughter from a previous relationship, but seeing the look on his face anticipating the birth of Jersi made me smile. With that being said there was no way I was going back to P.A. Mom didn't agree, but she gave me her blessings, said she had washed her hands with me, took my sisters and left.

Jon and I moved in together and things actually weren't that bad. He worked while I stayed home and prepared for Jersi. I knew him like the back of my hand so I knew everything that made him tick. So I didn't go outside and when I did I dare not look in another man's direction. Jon was so insecure. I was super pregnant and ready to burst yet and still he was afraid of losing me. The only thing I never got used to was him forcing me to have unwanted sex with him. He hated rejection, but it wasn't fun or enjoyable for me anymore. I was literally only there because I didn't want a broken family. I had enough of that shit in my life. I finally came to my senses in my eighth month of pregnancy. I knew if I had Jersi in Texas he would drive me crazy and/or do some dumb shit so I started formulating an escape plan.

    I called my dad and told him what was going on, and with no questions asked he got me a plane ticket for two weeks out. My mom secured me a ride to the airport and I knew Jon had to work so this was going to go smoothly.

    I gradually started packing my clothes everyday while he was at work and hiding suitcases in the closet. I was watching the calendar like a kid waiting for Christmas, and wouldn't you know it; when the day came for me to leave this bitch calls of work. My heart was beating out of my chest, but there was no turning back now I got too many people involved.

    He was sitting on the couch, and I'm in the room talking to myself sounding just as crazy as he was. I suddenly remembered that he had a gun in the closet and always threatened to kill me if I tried to leave him. So I called the police, explained the situation, and asked them to come escort me safely out of the house. They said they would be there shortly, but that seemed like it took hours. My ride was outside, and I was pacing back and forth wearing a whole in the damn carpet with my big pregnant ass. Finally the police came, and knocked on the door. Jon was surprised as shit when he opened it and the burst in and told his crazy ass to sit down somewhere. They came in the bedroom and helped me with my bags. Jon was livid. I can only imagine that if they wasn't cops he was definitely goin out shooting.

"Where are you going with my baby? Why are you doing this to me?" he cried.

I immediately felt bad, but I had to go or he was literally going to be the death of me.

"I'll be back Jon. I just have to leave for a while." I lied.

That was the last time I ever saw Jon.

CHAPTER 9

Not long after my great escape I gave birth to Jersi. We call her Jersigurl. She came into this world as if she had been here before. She had beautiful black hair, with red Indian like skin. She had light brown eyes; such a beautiful baby. The most beautiful baby I had ever seen.

Jersi was such a good baby and I took her everywhere with me. Everybody loved Jersi and she was spoiled rotten. Let my mom tell it Jersi was her baby and not mine. At times I wished Jon was there, but I knew it was for the better that he wasn't. We talked from time to time, and he always begged me to come back. Then he always showed me that I made the right decision.

Six months after Jersi was born I was walking down the street going to get something to eat. By that time I was 18, drinking, smoking weed, and living life or so I thought. Yup! You guessed it again (boy ya'll are really getting good) a dude pulls up on me trying to holla at me. I knew he wasn't from around there and it turned out he was from Philly. So I'm listened to him kick his game. He asked me where I was going and I told him. I was shocked when the nigga peeled off $50 and told me that dinner was on him. Needless to say we exchanged numbers.

The next day he called and told me to get dressed because he was coming to get me. I didn't even hesitate to accept. I was truly intrigued by this man. By the way, his name was "L". I was sitting on my porch waiting from him, and I heard him bumping Jeezy a mile away. I was hype because he was good looking and of course older than me. He also wasn't around here so it that was a plus. When I jumped in he had a few blunts rolled up which excited me even more.

"You got a curfew?" He asked looking me in they eyes making me instantly wet.

"Nah. My mom got my daughter so we good."

He pulled off and we went to the city. We ate, drank, talked about life, his kids and my daughter. We talked about life goals, likes and dislikes etc.

"What you wanna do next?" he said paying for the expensive dinner.

"I wanna get a tattoo?"

I was bullshittin but he took me to the tattoo parlor.

"Get anything you want. Don't worry about the price."

I picked a butterfly with eyes around my name on my lower back.

"Great choice. Just so you know I'm always watching you." He said.

Daaaaaamn this nigga was smooth. I had died and gone to heaven.

When the night was over he dropped me off and left me with a few hundred dollars.

"Go get some nice stuff for Jersi in the morning."

My heart dropped. That was some real player shit I had to admit. He only met me today, and never met Jersi, but still did what he did. I was hooked.

That night I couldn't sleep. I just kept thinking about "L". The feeling must have been mutual because he called me and told me he was thinking about me as well, but that he desperately needed to talk to me about something. My heart was in my throat as I waited for him to pull up. I was already expecting the worst; shit the worst was all I had come to know in my life. I was damn near immune to the shit.

"What's good baby girl?" he said as he pulled up on me.

"Skip the formalities "L" what's the deal?" I said not in the mood for the fluff shit.

"Damn. Okay then I'll get right to it then."

"Yeah. I'd appreciate it."

"Okay look. I got a girl at home, but shit aint workin out, just bare with me and I'mma end that shit."

Yup just as I expected. At this point I just figured that I did something in my past life and God had it out for me. I was dying inside from the latest bullshit that was dropped on me, but I wasn't gonna show it.

"Nah nigga you aint gotta do that. Lose my number please." I said quickly turning before he could see the tears streaming down my face.

I hurried inside before my breakdown was evident. I was so sick of getting a taste of happiness just for it to be snatched away from me a short time after, and I'm also so tired of these chapters ending like this….aint ya'll …. But c'est la vie?

CHAPTER 10

Over the next few weeks I was starting to feel the way my mom used to. I was drinking heavy, wouldn't leave the bed, and had Bianca pretty much holding Jersi down for me. I know it sounds crazy because I didn't really know "L" at all, but what I saw in just those few hours lit a spark in my soul like I had never had before, and to have that all snatched from me in the blink of an eye was just too much for me. And just when my world seemed shattered and I thought there was no God "L" called me. I started not to answer. Truth is I actually tried not to answer, but my heart compelled me to do otherwise. I quickly got myself together and put on the biggest front ever.

"I thought I told you to lose my fuckin number." I snapped while still fighting back tears.

"Pack you and Jersi's things. I'm on my way to get ya'll and change ya lives." Was all he said before hanging up abruptly.

I stared at the phone and checked the call log just to make sure it was actually "L" that had called and not some random nigga with the wrong number. I couldn't believe what I had heard. I was dazed and confused. I had only met him once and then hadn't spoken to him in weeks after he told me about his girlfriend, now here he was calling me to pack up me and my daughters shit to move in with him? I don't know how long I laid there trying to process the situation, but before I knew it he was outside blowing the horn. I jumped up out the bed, quickly tried to get myself together to look presentable and ran downstairs.

"Where you and Jersi shit at?" He said getting out of the car and walking towards me.

"Yo "L" are you serious? I aint spoke to you in weeks, then you call out the blue and I'm supposed to just pick up and move me and my daughter into your house?"

"Yeah." He said without blinking an eye.

That shit made me wet instantly; so much that I aint even have a comeback   except..

"Okay. Let me pack our things."

"No need. I will just buy ya'll all new shit. Go get Jersi and I'll be in the car."

Who the fuck did this nigga think he was? My man that's who. I grabbed Jersi and did what I was told.

CHAPTER 11

Life with Jersi and "L" couldn't be better. I had fallen head over heels in love with this man. The way he treated me was one thing, but he treated Jersi as if she were one of his own. "L" had two sons that I totally adored; they would come down from Philly and stay the weekend with us. It felt weird at first because here I was holding down a total household and I was only 18. It was hard in the beginning because his even though I only saw his kids on the weekend they didn't know me, so it took some getting used to. "L" taught me the ropes and held my hand through it all.

No one really liked or understood the relationship between me and "L". His mother really didn't like her 31 year old grown man of a son was in love with and taking care of a young 18 year old girl. They really hated it when I became pregnant by "L" with yet another girl who we named Kailee; she was my yellow princess. Kailee was greedy as all hell and a true daddy's girl.

For the first time in my life I really felt like my life was complete. Although I was only 18 I had a true family. Jersi loved "L" and as far as she knew he was her dad, and as far as "L" was concerned Jersi was his daughter and may God be with you if you ever tried to tell him different. He loved Jersi so much that he went and got her name tatted on his arm. I truly could not and would not ask God for a better man.

If ya'll asses been paying attention then I'm sure you know by now that my life with "L" didn't stay all peaches and cream. I past made me fragile so it didn't take much for "L" to make me snap the fuck out on him or break down crying. "L" and I had plenty late night cheating confession talks. I guess in all honesty I expected him to cheat because he was so much older, and he expected me to cheat because I was so much younger. At first I would snap on "L" for his infidelities while hiding my own, but the one thing he taught me and drilled into my head was that we were friends first and could tell each other any and everything. So whenever we had our sexual slip ups we would tell each other. Yeah I know the shit is crazy ya'll shut up.

Throughout all the crazy shit we still had mad fun. We would throw parties and BBQ's at the house and invite a few people over. It took a while for "L" to even allow people at the crib because he was always cautious of who we kept around us and who we allowed to know where we laid our heads. He was almost militant with that shit, and I would like to think I played a hand in him being more sociable. He would open up more once he started sipping on Bacardi Limon. My mom put him up on that and he loved her for it.

My relationship with "L" was a strange one. It would get to the point where we would fight from one end of the house to the other, breaking everything in our path, then go out on the porch, smoke a blunt, look at each other laugh, say I love you at the same time, start cracking up, then end the night with the best make up sex in the world. Yeah, that was almost our daily routine.

<u>CHAPTER 12</u>

As much as the crazy shit "L" and I went through was cute in the beginning, by the time I was 21 I had grown tired of it and we were growing tired of each other. We were in the midst of splitting up when I got pregnant with my son Lee who was named after his father. We tried to make things work for sake of the children, but decided that if we were gonna salvage our great friendship it was best that we part ways amicably and on good terms before the damage was irreparable, so I moved back in with my mom.

Around this time "L" had started managing a barbershop, and we were still getting on each other's nerves. He was still a great dad from afar when he had time. "L" had tried a few times to reconcile and get things back to where they were with us, but by this time I had already moved on to my next headache; this nigga named 50. 5He was a good dude but he came with more drama and lies than the law should allow. He definitely had me out of element. With all the shit ya'll have read about me so far I was never out there fighting bitches over no nigga. I should have cut and run from the first fight, but I was still naïve as hell.

It was about 2 weeks before Valentine's Day 2011 when "L" came to the house to tell me that he missed me, and wanted his family back.

"Look Brook. I've changed and all I wanna do is make shit right between us. I want you and the kids back. I want my family back; I need my family back." He said staring me in the eyes with the utmost sincerity.

I loved "L" but I wasn't really tryna hear none of that shit. Since our break up he had built up a huge fan base of bitches and drama. I was taking enough of that shit from 50 and I just couldn't and wouldn't deal with anymore of it.

"L" we been through this a zillion times. We are better off as friends and co-parents; no more and no less. So let's not fuck up a good thing okay?"

"Okay fine. Well before I go I want you to remember these two very important things. First, if anything ever happens to me I want you to look at (I won't say his name) and second if that day should come; you are gonna miss me when I'm gone. I love you Brooklyyn. Take care of yourself and my kids."

For the first time ever, I saw him hang his head low as he turned and left.

CHAPTER 13

February 14th 2011; Valentine's day I woke up to my sister screaming and a missed call from "L". It was 3am and all I remember is my sister telling me "L" was dead; he had been killed. I heard what she said, but still couldn't register what she was saying. It still hadn't hit me so I sort of had an out of body experience when I ran upstairs to tell my mom what happened.

I called 50 to have him take me over to the West Side. I still had not shown any emotions over the tragic news that I had just received. My stomach was hurting so bad yet I was still in denial. "L" wouldn't die on me, he would never leave me in this world by myself, and he would never let anybody get the drop on him. So the thought of some hatin ass nigga catchin him lackin made me disbelieve the story even more. I had to see for myself.

As we approached the barbershop I saw police and yellow tape everywhere. My head instantly started spinning as I ran up to the shop and saw his legs sticking out of the blood soaked sheet that they had draped over his body.

"WHY THE FUCK IS HE STILL LAYING HERE?" I yelled to the top of my lungs with my eyes still dry as bad cornbread.

Just then it hit me.

"KAILEE!" I screamed again realizing she had stayed with "L" that night.

I ran full speed to his house while silently reminding myself not to scare the kids when I got there.

"Keep it together for the kids Brook." I kept telling myself.

When I got to his house there were so many people there, and they all started staring at me as I walked in.

"Where's my daughter? Where are the boys?" I screamed referring to Kailee and his sons that stayed the night.

When the kids heard my voice they all came running.

"It's gonna be okay ya'll." I said not sure if I was trying to convince them or myself.

"L" and I had our differences but at the end of the day he was my best friend, my first true love, the father of my children, and the man who taught me everything I need to know. Now he was gone, and I couldn't believe it. Not to sound cliché' but when he died he took a piece of me with him.

I was in such a daze I never felt everyone's arms around me trying to console me.

"Get the fuck off me. Stay the fuck away from me." I said grabbing Kailee and leaving.

As far as I was concerned despite what "L" told me, everybody was a suspect and I wasn't fuckin with none of em. All I kept thinking about was the fact that his boys will grow up angry, Lee would never know his father (he was only 2 weeks away from his 1rst birthday), Kailee will never understand what happened; she was just laying on his chest right before he went outside, and Jersi just lost the only man she knew as her dad. What would I do without my other half? I miss him to this day, and I still cry at times while calling for his name. I wish he was here to see how big the kids have gotten. How big the boys got and how beautiful the girls are.

"I miss you "L" and will always love you and keep you in my heart."

CHAPTER 14

After losing "L" my life took a drastic change for the worse. I started drinking out of control, smoking heavy, hanging with the wrong crowd, and constantly running the streets. I even started bartending and stripping to make ends meet. It's crazy because in the blink of an eye I went from never having to want for nothing to rubbing two sticks together to survive.

Things had gotten so bad that I started hanging with these white girls that sniffed coke. That was never my twist, but one day I was curious.

"What does it make you feel like when you do it?" I asked nervously.

"It makes you feel numb." Becky responded taking a bump.

That's all I had to hear. I needed to be numb to ease the pain, to make it all go away. So I tried it and I loved it. It instantly made all the pain, loneliness, and sorrow go away. Depending on who you asked, some would say I loved it too much, but what the fuck did they know? Some of them are reading this right now. Did ya'll go through what I went through? No? Okay I aint think so. Fuck outta here with ya'll holier than thou judgmental, hypocritical asses. Talkin shit but still reading huh? Ya'll hoes kill me, but I digress.

****
****

As only my luck would have it my mom started getting sick again out of nowhere. And once again nobody knew what was going on. She was losing so much weight it was crazy. In the middle of all that this crazy lady went and had another baby; my brother Riccar. I aint even know she was pregnant, none of us did; it shocked the hell out of everybody.

To be totally honest with you, Bianca and I were not happy with mom having another kid. I had my own three kids to care for, my step dad Rick was working all the time and when he wasn't he was taking care of my mom so Bianca and I knew we had to step up and help with Little Ricky, but that shit was hard.

After mom ended up back in the hospital and the doctors still couldn't figure out what was wrong we didn't think mom would make it. Bianca and I were doing the best we could to take care of mom and keep the house afloat, but it truly started to become unmanageable. So my mom being the super woman that she is hired a nanny to help take care of us and the house.

Okay confession time. I never went to the hospital to see my mother. I know it sounds selfish, but I was still depressed and a whole mess from "L" and then everything else hitting me at once. With my mind all fucked up the way it was I just couldn't bring myself to see my mom in that condition. She was upset but she understood.

A few weeks later mom came home from the hospital. She was still a bitch tryna call shots all sick and shit. I would just laugh and shake my head like *mom sit yo ass down somewhere; we got this.* As Bianca got older her and mom would fight like cats and dogs. I tried my best to keep the peace, but Bianca had a mouth on her. I would hold stuff back but BeBe had no filter and no regards for anybody's feelings. I'll never forget one day her and mom was arguing about something small; I wanna say it was about Bianca cleaning the kitchen. Everybody knows a clean kitchen is one of mom's biggest pet peeve. Anywho, BeBe said something to piss mom off and she came charging up the stairs butt ass naked, sick and weak as shit. She mustered up all her strength, picked Bianca's T.V. up over her head and threw that shit down the stairs. I was laughing so hard I had tears coming out of my eyes. There was never a dull moment on Washington St.

CHAPTER 15

As the months went by I hadn't changed a bit. I was still drinking, drugging, and partying. One night I was on a mission headed to one of the neighborhood bars. I decided to go to one of the white bars because that's where all the ballers went because the white spots had the best clients. I was on my way in when this dude passed me on his way out.

"Yo. Don't go nowhere. I'll be right back aight?" He said.

I looked around to see who he was talking to.

"Who me?"

"Yeah you. I'll be right back."

I swear I had never seen this man a day before in my life, but I was like okay whatever, and just went inside to enjoy myself. I sat at the bar and was downing shots when the same dude walks in 20 minutes later. He spotted me at the bar and immediately made his way over to me.

"Gotdamn this nigga smell good." I thought to myself.

He was definitely a looker. He had smooth milky way skin, freshly done shoulder length dreads, Armani shirt and Jeans, jewels, the works. Whoever this nigga was he looked and smelled like money.

"You Brooklynn right?" He said flashing a smile that sent chills through my body.

"Yeah. Who are you?" I asked, wondering how this dude knew me.

"They call me Brick Man. I tried to talk to you a while ago, but you curved the shit outta me. Talkin bout you had a dude or something like that."

Ahhh this must have been when I was fuckin with 50. Oh well, that was then and this was now. I let Brick Man sit down as we drank and chopped it up all night.

"You wanna get outta here and go chill at my people's crib?" he asked.

"Sure. Why not?" I responded as I watched him peel off and pay the large bar tab.

We ordered some take out and went to chill. We talked, and talked all night. Surprisingly enough he seemed a little shy, meanwhile my mouth was running a mile a minute. I got the feeling that he aint trust people like that, but I was used to his type; I had seen it a million times before.

He was a little more talkative over breakfast. I was actually surprised he was such a gentleman and didn't try to fuck me that night. After we ate we went our separate ways and he said he would hit me up, and a few days later he did. Being around Brick Man was like a breath of fresh air. When we were together we were always laughing, joking ad having a great time. I loved every bit of it, because I had not had that feeling in a very long time. When I was with B.M. I was on cloud nine. Whenever I was in his presence I didn't need to drink, smoke, or get high, because he was my natural high. His touch made me jump, his kisses made me melt, and the sex was amazing. The part I liked most was the fact that I could take him out of his element. When he wasn't in business mode he wasn't shy, or guarded; he felt free.

<u>CHAPTER 16</u>

Now after 15 chapters ya'll nosey motherfuckers know this shit aint last long. The story of my motherfuckin life right? Anyway after months of being together Brick Man had started being a little distant. I guess shit started getting old, like every other situation I was in, and to top things off Brick Man had caught a charge and was expecting to do some real time. We decided to stick it out and try to make things work in the meantime. The bright spot in my life was I was going to dental school and doing something positive with my life. This is the type of good shit that Brick Man brought out of me. When I finished dental school the look on his face was priceless; he grinned from ear to ear, but even that moment was short lived.

Soon after my graduation B.M. started wanting to spend less and less time together. It came out of nowhere. It's like he wanted to mentally prepare me to be without him when he got sentenced. I was crushed. Once again someone I cared deeply about was leaving me. One day he gave me some bread to go do something nice for myself. So to let him know exactly how I felt I went and got his named tatted on my pussy. I can't even begin to describe the look on his face when he saw it, and I refuse to go into detail about what he did after that (lol).

When the inevitable happened and B.M. was sent away that was kind of like the beginning of the end. I mean we tried to keep it tight, but he ultimately told me that he wanted me to live my life. He explained that he couldn't do his time worried about what I may or may not be doing in his absence so he decided to just dead the whole thing. A short chapter for a short relationship. What the fuck ya'll want from me?

CHAPTER 17

I eventually went back to bartending. It was just my luck that 50 started hanging out there every night. One night he came with some dude that was a fucking menace. He looked like trouble as soon as I saw him, and I despised this nigga right of the rip. Regardless of the fact that 50 and I was no longer together I still loved him and vice versa. I used to tell him that hanging with that dude was gonna end him right back in jail. I found out later that the trouble makers name was Bump. Bump was like a wild animal that was just let out of a cage. His actions were indicative of a nigga who just came home from doing 8 years; so that explained it all. I had seen the bar kick niggas out for a lot less than the shit Bumpy was doing, but they had nothing but respect for this nigga for some reason.

I had started doing day shift at the bar and Bumpy would come in, have one beer and never finish it. I tried not to even look his way; he was creepy and scary. He was short, dark skinned, with a Sunni beard , muscles that had they own muscles and waves outta this world. He was actually a cutie, just too crazy for my liking, not to mention the fact that he was cool with my ex.

One day I wanted to smoke so I got the courage to ask him if he knew anyone that had anything. From watching how he moved he seemed very resourceful. He made a few calls and told me he had it covered.

"I don't smoke nothing but the best." I said meaning every word of it.

He smiled, which shocked me because I had never seen him do that before. There was something behind his smile that did something to me, but I quickly dismissed it.

Within minutes he made good on the smoke, and that started some very good dialogue between us. He actually started coming in during the day to just chop it up with me and keep me company. The more we talked the more I enjoyed his company. This customer from hell was actually pretty funny when he wasn't being a total dickhead.

Who knew the chance encounter with Bump actually started to forge a great friendship between us? He was cute and cool but it was nothing more than that. He would come in the bar with different bitches here and there, but I wasn't impressed. To be totally honest he aint seem to into them; it seemed more like a status thing.

One night Bump approached me and asked a favor.

"Yo Brook can you take my cousin home for me? He too bent to drive, and I'm too bent to drive for him."

"What? Hell no. I don't know that nigga. And he drunk too; aint no tellin what he night try and do to me." I said rolling my eyes.

"C'mon now Brook; you think I would put you in harm's way? I'll tell you what; I'll ride with ya'll if that makes you feel better."

Truth of the matter was aside from his cousin being a stranger, I really just aint feel like doin the shit, but I reluctantly agreed as long as Bump rode with us.

"Ya'll niggas come on cuz I'm ready to go." I said snatching my keys off the bar.

After dropping his cousin off Bump and I went to grab a quick bite to eat before I pulled up to drop him off at his crib.

"Welp good night homie." I said yawning and ready to take my as home and get in my bed.

"Look; it's late and you obviously too tired to drive all the way hone so why don't you just crash here for the night?"

"Naw I'm straight nigga. You think you slick." I joked half heartedly.

"Girl aint nobody worried about you. You can get you some sleep, besides I got work to do anyway."

I wasn't feelin it at all, but he was right. I was tired as fuck and pretty drunk myself for real.

"Aight nigga, but I swear you better not try shit or I'mma Lorraina Bobbit yo ass." I said joking, but dead serious.

Once inside the apartment he did the gentleman thing and prepared the bed for me. He then rolled up a nice big blunt and smoked out. Of course this nigga aint keep his word, he was undressed, layin next to me and trying me in no time at all. I reluctantly gave in because I was too tired to fight this nigga off all night. It was all good though; the five minutes he lasted came and went in a flash.

The next morning over breakfast I had mad jokes for that minute man nigga, that he really aint like so I chilled. That nigga was mad that I had something on him now. If word ever got out that big bad ass Bumpy was a minute man his reputation would be crushed so I never told anybody..oh shit I'm tellin millions of people now. Oh well.

The situation between me and Bump was cool. He was doin him, I was doin me and when we were together we did each other, and he always made sure I was good and well taken care of. I still didn't know what to feel about him yet. I knew he was a bad boy that ran the streets and would lay a nigga down in a heartbeat, but he had a huge heart that most people never got a chance to see.

I had a tendency of going back to the bar where "L" was at right before he got murdered. I would always get so emotional and break down. I would then call Bump and he could always hear the tremor in my voice and knew what was up. He knew I needed him and he didn't care who he was fucking, or doing business with he would drop everything and tell me to come through. I would pull up on him, lie on his chest and cry my eyes out. It felt so good for him to hold me, tell me he got me, and that he would always be there for me no matter what. Being with Bumpy took every ounce of my anxiety away. That's when I knew I loved him and he loved me. We still didn't have an official title for our situation, but that didn't matter to either of us.

One day I was drunk and really feelin myself so I pulled up to Bump's crib without giving him any notice. I let myself in and headed to his bedroom where I found him pounding out some random hood rat pussy. Under normal circumstances I would have just turned around, left and hit him up when he was free, but for some strange reason she wasn't just fuckin Bumpy the neighborhood man whore baller, in my eyes this bitch was fuckin my man and I wasn't havin it. Before they knew what was going on I had jumped on that bitch and pulled all that cheap ass yackie out of her head. I beat that bitch all the way downstairs and out the house, then headed back upstairs to deal with Bumpy's ass who was sitting on the bed smoking a blunt and laughing.

"Yo Brook what the fuck was that abo…"

He never got a chance to finish his sentence because I punched him right in the fuckin face. The smile on his face quickly turned to the same snarl I saw the first time I laid eyes on him at the club, but before I could process it and realize the potential danger I was in, I was picking myself up off the floor, bleeding from the mouth.

"Bitch are you out of your fuckin mind?" He said grabbin me by my neck.

"Get the fuck off me Bump?" I screamed.

"Get the fuck outta here until you get ya shit together. I don't know what type of time you on suddenly, but you better figure that shit out. Now kick rocks Brook." He screamed in my face with a venomous rage.

The crazy thing is that nigga was right; I was trippin. What the fuck was I thinking? I mean we wasn't technically together but everybody knew what the fuck it was, that's why whenever he had a bitch in his face and saw me coming he would dismiss her with the quickness, and I would reciprocate the same respect on my end. I guess this was our strange way of showing that we truly loved each other.

CHAPTER 18

That fight with Bumpy lasted all of an hour and a half. That nigga pulled up on me, took me back to his house and fucked me like never before. Oddly enough; I think me snapping like that turned him on more than it pissed him off. In a weird way that shit even brought us closer, because from that day on we were thick as thieves.

One night we took the kids out to eat and we had such a great time that we decided to make it official and exclusive. It only seemed right because the kids loved him and he loved them back just as much. Often times if we were all walking together my son Lee would make us all hold hands and say that we were all family. Shit like that made me cry tears of joy. After all the kids had been through I never thought they would take to another man the way they took to Bump. I also saw a side of Bumpy I had never seen before either. The last thing I ever expected from him was to be the family man/father figure type. He even started calling them "his" kids and I was loving this side of him, but this too would be short lived.

In keeping with my life's tradition it wasn't long before Bumpy and I were fighting like cats and dogs, but this fighting was like no other fighting I had been through before. Bumpy would have his "black out" moments where he would just snap for no reason and then forget what the fuck he snapped out about. I was no angel; I'm sure I provoked a small portion of it, but this nigga was truly shot the fuck out. His temper was truly toxic; and not just to me, but to anyone who caught him on a bad day. I loved Bump, and after what happened to "L" I was super over protective of him. I couldn't stand to lose another man in my life, so whenever I saw him starting to act out in the bar I would tell him it was time for us to go.

Our relationship was complicated due to the trust issues we had with one another more so because of the way we met each other. As time went on I became more trusting of him, and he became the total opposite. He was more jealous, more possessive, and that caused his acts of aggression. It got to the point where he didn't even want me bartending anymore. He complained about me being too friendly with the customers. I always thought he was just over reacting until one night we were driving home from the bar and all was well or so I thought.

"Let me ask you a question Brook; do you think I'm some type of sucker ass nigga?" Bump asked looking back and forth between me and the road while he drove.

"OMG what the hell are you talkin about now Bump?"

"All up in niggas faces and shit all night like I aint even fuckin sittin there."

"Are you fuckin serious? I was doin my job Bumpy."

"Just doin ya job. You always blaming it on that fuckin job. If you was dead we wouldn't have that problem now would we?"

Before I could process what the fuck this nigga had just said he mashed on the gas and was trying to run us off the road into a brick wall.

"Yo you are really fuckin crazy. Stop this fuckin car." I said grabbing the wheel.

While trying to gain control of the car he slowed down just enough for me to open the door and attempt to jump out, but before I could undo my seatbelt he punched on the gas again. I had to hurry and close the door before it was taken off by a parked car.

"You aint nothing but a hoe ass bitch." He screamed as he drove with one hand and beat me in the face with the other.

"Bumpy stop before we get pulled over or you end up killing us both."

"You think I give a fuck about any of that shit?" He yelled damn near foaming from the mouth.

"What about the kids?" I screamed back with tears in my eyes.

It was the mentioning of the kids that brought him back to reality and caused him to slow the fuck down. For the rest of the ride he continued to yell, curse, call me every name in the book, and slap me, but he was driving like he had some damn sense and getting home to my babies was all that mattered to me. When we got home I ran inside to the kids, and Bump went straight to bed.

The next morning the kids and I were at the table eating breakfast. I had slept in there room in order to avoid any late night madness from the nutcase I called my man. And just as if I had summoned the dickhead with my thoughts he came walking into the kitchen. I secretly grabbed a knife, because whoopin my ass in private was one thing, but doing it in front of my kids was a whole 'nother violation and that shit wasn't goin down today.

"Good morning Bae. Morning kids. Babe what you feel like doing today?" He said giving me one of the most passionate kisses ever.

Who the fuck was this? Because it sure as hell aint the nigga that damn near killed me last night.

"Really Bump? You expect everything to ne all good after the shit you pulled last night?" I asked with an attitude?

"Hold up babe. What happened last night and what the fuck happened to your face?" He asked overly concerned.

"Aww this nigga is bi-polar." I thought to myself.

"Kids ya'll go to ya rooms and don't come out till I tell ya'll to." I instructed.

I waited for them to empty the kitchen then turned my attention back to Bumpy.

"Are you fuckin serious? You don't remember whoopin my ass on some ole nut shit?" I asked with tears of anger in my eyes.

"I did what? When? Why? No babe I don't remember any of that. I only remember coming to get you from work, and driving us home."

The look in his eyes said he was sincere, and that in itself was a problem. Violent blackouts could be dangerous and life threatening. I know that should have been my queue to leave but I couldn't bring myself to do it. No matter what his issues were I still loved him, and I couldn't leave him because he needed me now more than ever. The truth of the matter is when he wasn't trippin he was the backbone of our family and he acted accordingly.

CHAPTER 19

In an effort to get myself together once again I attempted to pursue my Dental career I kept getting doors shut in my face. As that good ole Brooklyyn curse would have it this white bitch I sold some coke to two fuckin years ago had set me up so now I had even more obstacles to overcome in my life; as if I need more of that shit. This junkie ass bitch set me up just so she wouldn't get charged. I swear I could have found this bitch and tortured her for days, but I let it go. She was gonna overdose and die anyway so fuck her.

To save myself from a jail sentence I told them devils that I was a user and not a seller. They fell for it hook, line and sinker so I copped out to a felony, a rehab program, and three years probation. To make matters worse Bumpy had also gotten himself in some trouble for bein the nut that he was so he had to go to jail for a year. I was sick to my stomach. Bumpy had made me stop working so with him gone there was no money coming in, so needless to say I ended up losing the house and me and the kids had to move back in with my mom until I figured some shit out. It was at this point that I really started resenting Bump for leaving me and the kids with nothing.

Without a pot to piss in or a window to throw it out of I resorted back to the thing I knew most; the streets. I went back to bartending, dancing, hustling, partying, and the whole nine yards. I was basically doing any and everything to make some bread besides selling pussy. Shockingly enough I was still communicating and talking to Bumpy. I wasn't faithful to him in the least, I tried to lie on our calls and visits but he could see right through my bullshit. We ended up breaking up, but vowed to stay in contact for sake of the kids; I would never take them from him no matter what.

A few months later I met this guy on Facebook. He was unlike any man I had ever dated. He had a real job with the school district, had a real schedule, and came home at a certain time every night. He was a really good guy with not an ounce of street shit in him. I figured he was good for me even though Bumpy still had a good portion of my heart on lock, but maybe it was time for a change and I didn't need to be with him. With all the damage we had done to each other maybe it was just best for me to move on and pursue something new with "S.M.".

S.M. and I dated for a while and things were going great. I even got the nerve to keep it real with Bumpy and tell him the truth. He wasn't too thrilled, but he'd rather me settled down than running the streets. Not to mention the fact that he swore up and down that he was getting his family back whenever he got home from jail. I paid him no attention because I had found out that he had a fuckin kid on the way.

Yeah the nigga was cheating on me and his dumb ass got the bitch pregnant. She just as dumb for keeping it thinking he was gonna be with her; you know the ole "keep a nigga baby". But that's a whole 'nother story I won't even get into. That bitch aint worth the ink on this page.

S.M. decided to move me and he kids in with him. They were "okay" with him, but they wanted their dad Bumpy. I explained that he would be home soon. They liked S.M. but not on a dad level. He was just like the goofy friend, the homeboy. He never crossed the lines, and never tried to fill their dad's shoes. He took his time with them and I loved that.

We decided to do take a huge leap and get married. At this point in my life there was nothing I wanted more. I knew we were rushing it, but I also figured that maybe this is what I needed to be complete in God's eyes. When I told Bumpy about our plans to get married he was livid.

"I allowed you to fuck around with this dude until I got home. Now you gonna go and marry this square ass nigga Brooklynn?" Bumpy screamed during my visit with him through clenched teeth.

"First of all you aint allow me to do shit. And second of all how dare you try to run a guilt trip on me and you got a whole baby on the way. Boy bye." I said unfazed by his tantrum.

"Brook I'm only fucking with her so that she can pay for shit and hold me down in here since you left a nigga on stuck."

"You don't really wanna talk about leaving nobody with nothing Bump. And I don't give a fuck about the reason why you fuckin with her. There shouldn't even be a baby in the picture anyway. I did a lot of shit, we both did, but I was never stupid enough or careless enough to have a baby on you Bump."

"Look Brook shit happens."

"You right about that. I'll send you a wedding invite." I said getting up to leave.

I knew that last jab cut him deep; the pain in his eyes was evident. I would apologize for the pettiness at a later date, but right now I needed him to share and wallow in my hurt with me.

Meanwhile on the home front I didn't know what to make of the situation. Bumpy was my weakness and poor S.M. knew it. He turned a blind eye to me going to see Bumpy alone, and encouraged me taking the kids to see him. He even allowed Bumpy to call the house for me. For the first time ever in my life I thought my mate deserved more than what I was giving. The truth of the matter is I only had one foot in the relationship with S.M. and if we were supposed to get married that wasn't a good look so I spared him and broke it off. He respected me for that, and we still kept in touch because we truly did love each other. I was just too fucked up in the head to give him all of me, and a good man like S.M. deserved nothing less. Aint that a bitch. The first time I get a good man in my life, I give him back to the universe so that HE can find someone better than ME.

CHAPTER 20

After breaking up with S.M. I started to go and visit Bumpy more frequently. I knew he was still seeing his baby's mother because she was taking care of him financially, and I was cool with that because I had too much shit on my plate to be parting with any type of bread.

I went to see Bump for his birthday, and this visit was one like no other. We were sitting there talking about life, how much we missed each other and how we were going to put our family back together by any means necessary. Hearing the sincerity in his voice and seeing the sincerity in his eyes had me in my glory, but while looking into his eyes they suddenly went from a look of sincerity to a look of fear.

"Happy Birthday Bumpy." His baby mother said sitting down.

This was about to turn into one hell of a visit.

"What the fuck are you doing here?" He responded with venom that I was all too familiar with.

"I told you I was coming" she answered nonchalantly.

"And I told yo ass not to come." Bumpy barked while banging his fists on the table and causing a scene big enough to have everyone including the guards look our way.

"Everything alright over here?" One of the guards said as he walked over to our table.

"Yeah we good over here." I said verbally shooing the guard away.

In case you haven't figured it out yet the upstate facilities allowed up to 3 visitors at one time, so that's how this bitch was able to prance her nappy headed ass over to our table unannounced.

"Well since we all here let's go ahead and put things into perspective." I said crossing my legs with an evil grin.

"Chill out Brook." Bumpy said knowing me well enough to know I was about to get on my super petty shit.

"Chill my ass. Tell her what the fuck it is." I said now raising my voice slightly.

"Yeah Bumpy tell me what the fuck it is." She said now crossing her legs.

"Look this aint the time or the place for this shit." He said while flicking his thumb and forefinger back and forth like he always did when he was in deep thought.

"Bumpy if you want your family back you will set this bitch straight right here, right now, for good.

He was about to be combative but saw the look in my eyes and thought better of it. He turned to shorty and gave her the news.

"Look, I really appreciate all you have done for me, and I will always be there for my child, but I have always been honest with you about my love for Brooklynn; I never hid that from you. With that being said I'm rebuilding my family so you and I are ending this today."

She looked my way and started to open her mouth, but I closed it real quick.

"Bitch don't say a word to me. I been told yo ass that a baby don't keep no man. I tried to save you from this very moment a million times, but you aint listen so now you gotta deal with that hurt and embarrassment I'm sure you're feeling in the pit of your stomach right. Like he said the baby will be well taken care of. Good day." I said reading and dismissing her at the same time.

She looked towards Bump.

"Don't look at me. You heard her; you gotta go." He said sternly.

Damn that shit sent chills through my body, although I did feel kind of bad for her. I didn't blame her for falling in love with him. She was young, simple minded, and had his child. However I refused to let her have my man and now she knew this.

"I don't have a fuckin ride Bumpy. I got dropped off here."

"Are you fuckin serious?" We both said at the same time.

So here goes the weirdo shit; don't you know this space cadet sat there the whole 8 hour visit with us as we laughed, joked, reminisced about old times, old sexual escapades, and the whole nine. We went for a walk and everything and just pretended she wasn't even there. The shit was crazy.

CHAPTER 21

Bumpy was released a year later and we were immediately at each other's throats, so in true Brooklyyn fashion I ended up fucking up because he was running the home like a fucking military prison, and I couldn't and wouldn't take that shit. So during this time you know his salty ass baby mother was sitting there waiting on him. He would often go running to her when were on the outs, but that shit never lasted and her dumb ass kept taking him back, each time with hopes of him staying. Wrong again bitch.

In all honesty Bumpy wasn't the only one that went running when things got bad. I started calling S.M. again and he would come to my rescue each and every time. I had to call him one time because Bumpy had choked me the fuck out, and S.M. didn't hesitate to get to me as fast as he could to remove me from the situation. I felt sorry for him to because he kept thinking that each time he saved me would be the last time and he and I would eventually be together, but that never happened.

Staying with Bumpy was crazy and I knew it, but ya'll been reading along so you know by now that nothing in my life is normal. Yeah Bumpy had gotten violent, but I wasn't always on the receiving end. That nigga done got his mouth and head busted wide open on more than one occasion fucking with me.

The craziest thing we ever did was wake one February 5th and decided to go down to the Covenant House. Yeah yeah shut up bitches; I now it was stupid. I just figured that having me as his wife would make him feel more secure and calm his ass down, but that shit aint work. After the marriage he got even more controlling, more abusive and more crazy. So needless to say the marriage certificate proved to be nothing more but lies written on some poor dead tree that gave its life for the greater good; not this bullshit.

During the time we were going through our shit I had started these drug and alcohol classes. One of the girls in the class was going off one day as she looked at her phone. I was wondering what the fuck she was tripping off of. Come to find out there was an app she had on her phone where she could track her husband's text messages, phone calls, any websites he visited, and even his GPS location. Even though I knew I shouldn't have fucked with it, but I asked her to show me how to use it. I put that shit to use as soon as it downloaded. Come to find out this nigga was this nigga was really wildin' out. I was confronting his ass left and right and he had no idea how I knew so much shit. The mystery of it all was fun at first; until I found out he was fucking the neighbor. The thing that pissed me off was this bitch smiled in my face every day, asked about the kids, could she borrow milk and sugar. You know; regular bum bitch neighbor shit. And don't let me even get started on the dozens of young bitches he was layin dick to. I swear he lucky I aint kill him in his motherfuckin sleep.

I just let a lot of shit rock, because when he was home he was home he was home and not trippin he was the poster boy for a great husband and father. We had date nights, family nights, and movie nights with the kids; it was heaven whenever it happened. When we wasn't tearin each other's heads off the kids loved him till no end. Jersi would always tell us she was going to run the family and be President one day. Bumpy would always say he loved her brain. Kailee was his Princess. He was so gentle with her. She was fragile and gentle and he treated her as such. She loved Bumpy so much. To this very day they have this thing where he says..

"You're not giving my what away?"

And she would respond.

"Your sugar and cream."

Then he would kiss her on both her cheeks. That would just tickle her pink. She would just lay across his chest for hours at a time. I'm pretty sure her attachment to Bumpy came to him filling the male void in her life after "L" was murdered. Now Lee on the other hand never got to meet "L" or get to know him for that matter so he looked up to Bumpy. He always strived to make Bump proud of everything he did from boxing to acting to whatever. Lee would call himself running the house whenever Bump wasn't home, because Bump would tell him that he was in charge in his absence. Lee took that shit to heart and ran with it lol. Those were the times I loved.

When the kids were around Bumpy would always be on his best behavior so this way when I snapped on him for some shit he had done I always looked like the bad guy smh, and whenever the kids were gone he would start his shit back up.

One night he came home late from the bar where niggas had been filling his head with lies about what I was doing behind his back while he was locked up. These Joe ass niggas just thought they was givin him lies and gossip not knowing that the mere inkling of any infidelity was his trigger. So that night he came home picked a fight and proceeded to whoop my ass. These actions were not new to me, but this particular night Bumpy took it a step further. This crazy motherfucker wrapped a chain around my neck and dragged me through the house kicking, screaming, and gasping for air. He was simultaneously kicking, punching, and slapping me the entire time, but wasn't no weak bitch; I refused to cry in front of him. Instead I fought back with all of my might until he got tired of dragging me and I passed out from lack of oxygen.

When I came to after passing out I had to smoke a blunt, and about a quarter of the way through the blunt is when I started to cry.

"What the fuck are you doing to yaself Brooklynn?"

"Why do you keep putting yaself in these fucked up situations?"

"When are you goint to break this fucked up cycle you have been going through for years?"

These were the questions I kept asking myself over and over as tears flooded the shores of my face. I needed relief, even it were only temporary. So I called the only person I knew would come running to save me; I called S.M. who had loved me enough to move right up the street from me and Bumpy so that he could be close in case of emergency. I grabbed my cell phone and dialed his number.

"I'm on my way baby." Is all he said when he picked up the phone.

Minutes later I was in his arms, crying my eyes out as we watched T.V. in his bed. I loved him because he never once said *"I told you so."* or rubbed my poor decision making and choices in my face. I especially loved the fact that he always respected me and never tried to fuck me. I know he wanted to take me away from it all and give me the life he knew I deserved, but he also knew that if Bumpy found out about our secret rendezvous' sexual or not he would kill us both. So we just kept things the way they were while praying that we never got caught.

CHAPTER 22

In the midst of all the bullshit my mom had moved back to Texas which was good because as time passed I had stopped crying over my situation. I had actually taken my tears and forged them into hatred for the man I married. So I planned a trip to Texas without his knowledge and I left his ass. I left because he was making me weak and I no longer knew who Brooklyyn was anymore. When I washed my face in the mornings I didn't even recognize the broken woman in the mirror. I had left my kids back home with their Aunt's so they were in good hands. I just needed a breather, I needed a change of scenery to get my mind right.

I didn't tell my family what I was goin through with Bumpy because when I went back to him I didn't want them hating my husband. I knew I would go back because I was a fool in love no matter what he put me through. I was determined to make things work no matter what it took.

I had been gone for about two months, and while I knew Bumpy was still at home doing the same old shit I also knew that he was drowning without me. As weird as it may sound I kept him balanced; without me in his life he was destined to end up in a casket before his time. Through our conversations on the phone I could hear in his voice how miserable he was without me and the kids. He missed his family like crazy and we missed him too. I explained to him that all I wanted him to do was treat me right on a consistent basis. He swore on everything God created that he would do just that. The next day he flew me back to Pennsylvania to start life over and do things the right way.

When I landed he was so happy to see me. He hugged me, kissed me, and begged me to never leave him again. The one thing he failed to mention was that in all of his promises and crying he still had not gotten his hoes in check. So not even 48 hours after my return we were at it again. I felt so hurt and stupid. Why the fuck did I even come back? I had found out that with all the shit Bumpy had put me through, the shit I learned when I got back home was unforgivable and I will just leave it at that. At this point all I needed to do was carefully plan an exit strategy. Ever since I dipped on him out of the blue and went to Texas he was on my heels heavy. So just up and running was out of the question. I had to be smarter and more calculated this time; but how?

They say if you are not moving fast enough for God then he will speed the process up for you. One night Bump and I actually argued ourselves to sleep. I don't even remember what it was about, all I know it was serious enough for us to argue all the way until we dozed off.

In my sleep all I could hear were feet running up the steps, and before I could gather my thoughts the police had kicked in our bedroom door. It was a fuckin raid, and with all the shit they had on Bumpy needless to say my husband has been gone ever since.

CHAPTER 23

Bumpy was sentenced to 12 years, he has been down only 3 so far, but we are praying for an appeal. With Bump on lock it was time for me to start being the bread winner in the family again. So once again I revert back to all I know; the streets. I had moved back to Philly because I knew I could make a hell of a lot of money there. I was hustling and getting my hands on every type of drug the ballers wanted. I was pretty, sexy, thick, street smart, and I had drugs. Who wouldn't wanna fuck with me on any level? My name was ringin bells in Philly. If I wasn't dancing, or sling drugs a mile a minute I was politicking with rappers and being the featured girl in all of their videos. The first video I ever did was for my girl Nat from Mob Wives. I was super hype to meet her. She was so thorough and equally as sweet; I love Nat.

Aside from getting to the money I had started to develop a relationship with my biological father. Things were going well between us and he would often let me stay the night whenever I was in the city late. Even though he was never there for me when I was young, he was there for me now and that was all that mattered. It actually felt so good to be around him, and I was loving every minute of it.

I eventually ended up getting a job as a Hookah Girl, at one of the most lit clubs in the city. I had met a lot of people and was giving my number out mostly for entertainment purposes. I had been working there for about a month and there was a guy who I met there that used to blow my phone up. I had him stored in my phone as "E". I never answered his calls or texts; like I said I mostly gave my number out for entertainment and never returned any calls or texts so I was confused as to why I even had his numbered stored in the first place.

One day I was chilling with my girl Lovey. We was smoking, and watching T.V. before I headed out to my hair appointment. I had just passed her the blunt when my phone rang from a number I didn't recognize.

"Hello?"

"Yo what's good? This is "E". You gave me ya number while ago but I cant ever get a hold of you."

Yo this nigga was crazy. He gonna call me from a different number because I be ignoring the calls from his phone.

"Oh hey. What's up?" I said trying not to sound as fake I was really being.

"Aint shit. What you doin?"

"I'm about to order my Uber to go to my hair appointment."

"C'mon now stop playing with me. I got money, weed, molly's, perks whatever you need. I'mma scoop you up and take you where you need to go."

I was like *"Fuck it. If he gonna give me all of that and save me some money with Uber, then why not let him swing through?"* So I gave him the address and waited patiently for this mystery man to show up. The crazy shit is I didn't even remember what he looked like at all, but according to him I would find out in about 20 minutes.

When we got to the salon "E" gave me some weed, some money and a Percocet and told me to call him when I was done so he could come pick me up. "E" was definitely my type of guy; the one you didn't have to give instruction to, because he knew just what to do and when to do it. Ever since that day we have been together everyday tripping, smoking, joking, and enjoying life.

CHAPTER 24

Although I enjoyed his company I didn't take "E" too seriously. After all I had been through including a failed marriage I would just play the games that niggas played. My friend Sean (you'll get to know him later) has a saying. *"Do it to em first, and do it to em worse"*. That was a code he lived by in order to protect himself from anybody he thought may be out to do him dirty and the shit really works for him so I adapted the same code.

Truth of the matter is I wanted to give "E" a shot at the title, but after he told me that he was in a "situation" with his kid's mother I really fell back and decided to accept whatever we had for whatever it was. I was really cool with that and wasn't really beat for anything else. However....

After a few months of being together so much "E" and I started to develop strong feelings for each other, but I still couldn't let him in I just really loved his friendship and I was dealing with this rapper at the same time. The rapper just didn't have enough time for me between traveling, recording etc. So I found myself lonely a lot more than I wanted to be. "E" on the other hand was always there for me no matter what; he became my best friend.

I had a trip that came up for a modeling job in Puerto Rico and "E" supported me big time. I wasn't surprised though because he supported me with any and everything that made me a better woman, person and mother. Had my prayers finally been answered?

Slowly but surely "E" and I started becoming way more than just friends, but what the hell was I thinking? Due to Social Media his baby mama found out where he had been spending all of his time at, and of course she didn't like it. I was never one to be a home wrecker, but "E" wasn't making it easy on me. He knew me too well, he knew everything I loved, and I just couldn't let him go so I made him my manager to keep him around for "business purposes".

That shit aint work out too well. His baby moms ended up calling me one day and we spoke like two adult women. I couldn't hold back anymore and I told her everything. After I did it I felt relieved and bad at the same time so I did the womanly and respectful thing and stayed away from "E".

The "keep away from E rule" lasted about three months, and then we re-connected and picked right back up where we left off. We are not together, but he is close enough to me to be whatever he wants. He protects me, takes care of anything I need, and I do the same for him.

CHAPTER 25

I was having so much fun in the streets that I started taking my Probation Officer for granted and she violated me for smoking weed. On top of that I also missed court so she issued a warrant for my arrest. And as if that wasn't bad enough I met this dude through an old boyfriend who asked me to rent him a car. I aint know the nigga so I said no, but then he asked me to meet him in person and feel him out in order to feel more comfortable.

I reluctantly agreed to meet up with him, and after he agreed to lace me with some money and some Percocet's I was all in. Well let me not make it sound like I only did it for drugs and money. After meeting him he was actually cool. He was cocky, had a Jamaican accent and a New York swag. He was also kind of cute, but not my type. I also knew that if he was cool with my ex that he had to be a thorough nigga.

We went on this app called Turo where people rent out their own vehicles so you could get anything from a hooptie to a Lamborghini and super affordable too. Homeboy was hype because all he had to do was deposit money into my account, click a button and presto the next thing you know he was in a drop top BMW. Everything went smooth and according to plan. He paid me what he said he was gonna pay me and brought the car back on time. So naturally when he asked to do it again I had no problem with it, but this time the motherfucker never brought the car back. I mean we were texting back and forth and he kept giving me the run around. First he was out of town, and then he claimed he parked it. I was so confused, and disturbed by this shit that it was stressing me out. I already had my probation hovering over my head, and I knew this was gonna be another charge because the car was in my name. I had the owner of the car calling me, I had detectives calling me. I told everyone what happened and that I was trying to find the car too. I had to get low until this shit blew over.

CHAPTER 26

I decided to take to take my kids and their cousins to a sleep over at a hotel. Things were going great, everyone was having fun and we were all happy. It warmed my heart to see the kids enjoying themselves until around 2am there was knock on the door.

"Open up it's the police."

Before I could react they were already in the room.

"Ms. Johnson we have a warrant for your arrest."

I immediately figured it was from my Probation Officer, but then I was like nah, she wouldn't send nobody all the way to Philly to get me.

"Please don't do this in front of my children." Was all I could say as I fought back tears.

They were nice about it and told the kids that I had a parking ticket. I kissed my babies, and went outside. Once I got outside they cuffed me, took me to the station and explained that the warrant was for that fuckin car. I made some calls and got the kids straight.

I ended up staying the night until my local authorities made the trip to come and pick me up and take me back to my jurisdiction. I made bail and was still pissed off because this had absolutely nothing to do with me. I didn't steal the fuckin car, but once again I can't win for losing. After making bail I headed straight back to Philly to get my kids and go on about my day as usual.

After making sure they were good I retained a lawyer. I knew this shit was far from over and even called my P.O. to find out why the warrant that she issued didn't pop up when I was booked, and she told me it had nothing to do with that. I told her when my court date was and advised her that when I was done with court I would head straight back to her office to get things situated, but that didn't happen. Although my lawyer got the car shit waived my warrant actually popped up and they shipped my yellow ass straight to Chester County Prison. You gotta be fucking kidding me.

CHAPTER 27

I have been sitting here for almost 2 months now. They had me do a drug evaluation since my original violation was for the weed, fines, and missing court. I was cool with that since I knew I didn't have a serious problem. I figured I would just get an outpatient program, but I was wrong. When the prison detoxed me they found the Percocet's in my system and decided that I should be sentenced to long term rehab. These money hungry devils are money hungry and the state gets about 50 grand per inmate that they send to long term rehab.

Jail is full of weirdo's, but there are some cool bitches that I met and talk to. I be with this one white girl who be snappin out, and you never know when it's coming. I be laughing my ass off at her. One time she went completely off because somebody used her pencil. That's my bitch but she definitely aint got it all. We are planning a trip to Cali when we get out of here. She needs me to balance her the fuck out.

I find that a lot of these bitches in jail aint really about that life. They talk heat but don't really want no smoke. They know can't shit really pop off in jail so they play the tough role. On the streets the majority of them would be dog food and they know it. A few of these junkie bitches be trying me but I refuse to let them get me jammed up even more than I already am, but best believe I don't forget shit so if anybody really and truly violates me in here they better hope they never see me out there.

The funny shit is my husband Bumpy is locked up downstairs and still think he runnin shit. He still cursin me out through the toilets, because that how you communicate in here. Yes you scream into the fuckin toilets.

You see all types of females coming in and out of this facility. There is one butch/dyke that came in. She has dreads, dark skin, and the most intriguing eyes. We started talking when she asked me for a pen one day. Once I started finding different things about her attractive I just chalked it up to me being in jail too long. LOL! We actually started hitting it off with great conversation. She told me about her wife and her daughter and I told her about all the bullshit I had been through.

The more she and I talk the more my feelings are growing for her. I been with females before but it was always just some sexual fun; nothing more. I never even thought about being with a female at all. I was always taught that females were meant to be with men, and now these feelings were breaking the rules. I mean this is crazy. I find myself wondering how her touch would feel, and when I think about it my pussy gets extremely wet. I guess the good and safe thing is that in here we can't touch or do anything. I'm not sure where this is headed but I'm pretty sure she wants to turn me out. LOL.

As day go by in here I'm starting to see who is really rocking with me, and who really cares about me. I'm currently in a cell by myself. I did have a celly who was showing me the ropes with this jail shit but she was shipped to another county. The Correction Officers are pretty cool and for the most part they do their job so I have no complaints with them.

I don't think most would last if this were a real jail; it's actually more like a boot camp. No matter what it is, being locked up is making me appreciate the little things on the outside I took for granted including but not limited to, my freedom, kids, food, and my life. I leave for rehab in about 2 weeks and I swear this has got to be the longest 2 months ever. Trust me God; lesson learned. Soon enough I will be out of the system and doing whatever it takes to mend my broken bridges.

TO BE CONTINUED.....

Made in the USA
Middletown, DE
27 June 2023

33880559R00043